DONAVAN'S DISCOVERY...

It all began one morning at the breakfast table. Donavan was staring at the back of a cereal box when he noticed the word NUTRITION.

"Nuuu-tri-tion," he said slowly. He liked the way the word slid down his tongue and rolled off his lips.

"Mom," Donavan said, watching his mother pack his lunch. "Do you like the word nuu-tri-tion?"

"I don't know, I never thought about it before," she answered.

"Me neither, but guess what? I am going to start paying extra attention to words from now on. I bet there are trillions of words out there, words I've never noticed."

DONAVAN'S WORD JAR

Monalisa DeGross
illustrations by Cheryl Hanna

HarperTrophy®
A Division of HarperCollinsPublishers

Harper Trophy® is a registered trademark
of HarperCollins Publishers Inc.

The interior illustrations are done in graphite pencil,
touched up with Prisma pencil on Strathmore illustration board.

Library of Congress Cataloging-in-Publication Data
DeGross, Monalisa.
Donavan's word jar / by Monalisa DeGross ; illustrations by Cheryl Hanna.
p.   cm.
Summary: When the jar that Donavan keeps his word collection in fills up,
he finds a special way to give his words away and get something wonderful in
return.
ISBN 0-06-020190-8. — ISBN 0-06-020191-6 (lib. bdg.)
ISBN 0-06-442089-2 (pbk.)
[1. Vocabulary—Fiction.]   1. Hanna, Cheryl, ill.   II. Title.
PZ7.D3643Do   1994   91-2470
[Fic]—dc20   CIP
                                                                 AC

First Harper Trophy edition, 1998

Visit us on the World Wide Web!
http://www.harperchildrens.com

15 OPM 50 49 48 47 46 45

To Donavan and his grandma
—M. L. D.

For Diane. Thanks for the laughter.
—C. H.

CONTENTS

DONAVAN'S WORD JAR

1

DONAVAN

Donavan Allen enjoyed being like all the other kids in Mrs. Panky's third-grade class. He liked wearing a yellow shirt with brown pants and a button-down sweater, just like the other boys. When the bell rang at the end of the day, he grabbed his book bag and ran for the door, just like the other kids. And just like the other kids, on the days when his mom packed raw broccoli and cauliflower in his lunch, Donavan forgot to eat them.

Like most of the kids in his class, Donavan liked to collect things. A few kids in his class collected rocks, insects, or stamps. Some other kids collected coins, comics, or baseball cards. Donavan's best friend, Eric, collected marbles. Eric was always playing marbles, trading marbles, reading about marbles, and searching for the perfect marble. He kept his marble collection in a leather pouch with his name stamped on it.

Donavan's buddy, Pooh, collected buttons of all shapes and sizes. Pooh kept his button collection pinned to a corkboard in his bedroom. He collected buttons from almost every event he

she
co
sects
marbles   stamps

attended. He had buttons from movies, baseball games, and amusement parks. Pooh's favorite button was the one his father had made for him for his birthday. On it was a picture of Pooh, and written around it were the words "Pooh for President." Pooh kept that button pinned to his book bag.

But when it came to collecting things, Donavan Allen was different. He had a collection like no one else he knew. Donavan collected words. Yes, words.

2

DONAVAN'S DISCOVERY

It all began one morning at the breakfast table. Donavan was staring at the back of a cereal box when he noticed the word NUTRITION.

"Nuuu-tri-tion," he said slowly. And then he said it again. "Nuuuu-trri-tion." He liked the way the word slid

down his tongue and rolled off his lips. This was a word he had never noticed before, and the word made him smile.

"Mom," Donavan said, watching his mother pack his lunch. "Do you like the word nuu-tri-tion?"

"I don't know, I never thought about it before," she answered, dropping a packet of raisins into his lunch bag.

"Me neither, but guess what? I am going to start paying extra attention to words from now on. I bet there are trillions of words out there, words I've never noticed."

On his way to school that morning, Donavan discovered the word BALLY-HOO blazing across a billboard.

"Wow! Was that there all the time?" he asked himself. And that same afternoon, he noticed the word BOUTIQUE written on the window of his mother's favorite shop.

"Gee, new words are everywhere," Donavan said. "Maybe I should start writing them down. I don't want to forget any of them."

That evening, while he was digging around in his father's tool chest, Donavan saw the word PINCERS written on a wooden handle. He pulled a strange-looking tool from the chest. It looked like a crab claw, and he laughed.

"This tool looks just like its name," Donavan said. "I wonder what it is used for. P-I-N-C-E-R-S," he spelled the word aloud to himself several times so that he would not forget how to spell it. Donavan went up the stairs and into his room, pulled his big dictionary from the shelf, and looked for the word PINCERS. "It does look just like a giant crab claw," Donavan said aloud as he looked at the page. "And just like a claw it can be used to grip things. This is great! From now on I am going to write my words down and keep them."

And so, Donavan began to collect words. He wrote his words in purple ink on yellow slips of paper. At the end of each day, he put the slips in a large, round glass jar. One day while Donavan was sitting at his desk putting words into his jar, he saw his little sister, Nikki, peeping around the door. He pretended not to notice her and kept writing down his words.

"What are you doing that for?" Nikki asked, leaning over his shoulder.

"Doing what?" was all he answered, and he kept on writing.

"Why are you putting those pieces of paper into that jar?"

"Because I collect words," Donavan said.

11

"Why?"

"Because I like the way they sound, and I want to keep them."

"Can I put one in?" Nikki asked, reaching over to pick up a slip of paper.

"No, Nikki. This is my collection, and it is private property. I don't want you messing with it." Donavan's voice was firm.

"Okay, Mister Meanie," Nikki said, leaving the room. "You'd better hurry, it's almost time for dinner." Donavan decided that he would keep his word jar high up on the shelf in his room. He didn't want Nikki snooping around his jar. She might break it or, even worse, take some of his words.

All kinds of words went into Donavan's collection. He had big words like PROFOUND that made him feel smart. Little words like CUDDLE warmed his heart. Donavan found that soft words like HUSH soothed his fears. Silly words like SQUABBLE slipped off his tongue and tickled his ears. From somewhere he collected HIEROGLYPHIC, a strange word that made him wonder. And just for fun, he added strong words like WARRIOR, words that rang in his ears like thunder. Donavan put mysterious-sounding words like EXTRATERRESTRIAL into his collection. And there were musical-sounding words like ORCHESTRAL.

Collecting words was fun—they were everywhere! One sunny Sunday afternoon Donavan found the word SOLIDARITY marching in a parade. He smiled at the men in their bright-green uniforms and wrote the word down. Later that same afternoon the word ZEPPELIN floated high in the sky, written on a silver balloon.

But Donavan's favorite way of collecting words was from people: people on the street corners, people in stores, people in the park, the people he heard on the radio, the people he saw on TV. Everywhere Donavan went, he listened; and he scribbled down new words.

Donavan collected so many words that his jar was jam-packed, filled to the brim, almost spilling over the rim, with words, words, and more words.

3

DONAVAN'S DILEMMA

One Friday morning Donavan was putting a word into his jar when he realized that there was no more room.

"I can't get another word in my jar," he said. Donavan went over and sat on his bed. He had a problem. "Maybe I should get a bigger jar," he thought.

"But then in a little while, I'll just have to get a bigger one." Donavan shook his head, "No, that won't work," he said.

"Donavan! Donavan!" He heard his mother's voice in the hall. "Come on, it's time for breakfast. What's taking you so long?" she called. "You'll be late for school."

"I'm coming right now." Donavan got up from the bed, grabbed his books from his desk, and ran out of the room.

When Donavan entered the kitchen, his mother was sitting at the table reading the paper. His breakfast was on the table.

"Mom, I've got a problem," Donavan said, as he put his books on the counter and then slid into the chair across from her. Donavan picked up his fork and began to eat his pancakes.

"There isn't space for another word in my word jar," he said between bites.

"You've collected that many words?" his mother asked. She sounded pleased.

"Yes," Donavan answered in a proud voice.

"Well, perhaps you should get a bigger jar," she suggested.

"Mom, I thought of that, but I'll only have to get an even bigger one when that jar gets filled." Donavan explained.

"You're right, Honey. Why don't you give this problem a little more thought? Maybe you'll come up with a better solution," his mother said, getting up from the table. "Don't forget to put your plate in the dishwasher. I'm going upstairs to check on your sister." Donavan watched his mother put his lunch bag on the counter next to his books. "Donavan, don't forget to eat the raw vegetables in your lunch," his mother said as she left the kitchen.

"Thanks, Mom," Donavan called out. Then he gathered up his books and lunch and started out for school. His mother was right. If he thought hard enough, maybe he could solve his problem.

That afternoon when school was over, Donavan decided to ask for Mrs. Panky's advice. She always seemed to have good ideas. He waited until everyone else left the classroom. He wanted to have all of Mrs. Panky's attention. Donavan walked over to Mrs. Panky. She was writing a list of presidents on the board.

"Hi, Mrs. Panky," he said.

"Hello, Donavan, are you staying after school?" she asked in surprise.

"I have a problem, and I thought

you could help me," Donavan said.

"Maybe I can. Why don't you give me the details."

Donavan told Mrs. Panky about his collection and explained his problem. When he finished she wrote on the board in big bold letters:

DONAVAN'S DEFINITIVE DICTIONARY

Mrs. Panky began to explain to Donavan all the things he needed to do to start his own dictionary.

"Mrs. Panky, that's going to take a lot of time, isn't it?" he asked.

"It certainly will," she answered in her best teacher's voice.

"Your idea is great, and I love that title, but I need a solution *now*," Donavan said.

"Well, why don't you think about it a little more?" Mrs. Panky suggested as she turned around and went back to writing on the board. "Donavan," Mrs. Panky added, "let me know what you decide."

That evening after Donavan finished his homework, he went downstairs to the basement to his father's workshop. He liked being in his father's workshop. It always smelled and sounded like important things were going on down there. His father was kneeling on the basement floor painting a long sign. His father used to work for a company that put new roofs on buildings. But in a week, he was going to open up a shop of his own. Donavan read the sign:

GREG'S ROOFING SERVICE
I'VE GOT YOU COVERED

"Dad, are you real busy?" Donavan asked.

"Not too busy, partner. I am just

starting to work on the sign for the new shop." Donavan watched his father carefully fill in the letter G with orange paint.

"Dad, do you think you're going to have your sign ready by the time your shop opens?" Donavan asked.

"Yes, I think I will. I plan to work on it a little every night. Is there something I can help you with, or are you just visiting?" his father asked.

Donavan explained his problem to his dad, and he told him about Mrs. Panky's suggestion. His father was quiet for a few moments and then he said: "Why don't you take Mrs. Panky's advice?"

"Dad, that idea would take too long," Donavan said impatiently. "Can you think of something I can do right now?" As Donovan talked, his father started to slowly fill in the letter R.

Donavan was about to ask his question again, when his father finally spoke.

"Partner, I think you should put those words in a shiny new file box. That way you could put them in alphabetical order, and whenever you needed a word from your collection you would be able to find it right away." Donavan's father looked at him and smiled.

"That's a good idea," Donavan said. "But won't I just have to get a bigger box when that gets filled?"

"Yes, I guess you would," his father answered, painting the letter E with a steady hand. "Well, maybe you'd better give it a little more thought," he suggested. "Sorry I can't help you."

"Don't worry about it, Dad." Donavan said as he walked up the stairs. "Good luck with your sign, Dad. It looks great."

4

DONAVAN'S DECISION

That night, lying in bed, Donavan thought about all of the suggestions he had heard that day. All of them were good ideas, but none of them solved his problem. He did not want to put his words in a book or a box. He liked

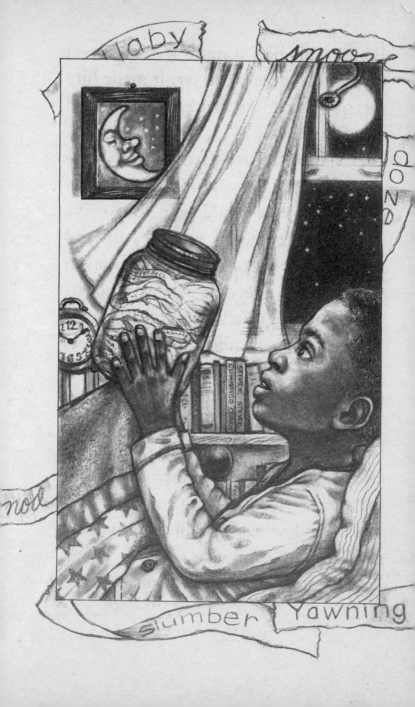

lying in his bed at night looking up at his words in the word jar. It made him feel good to know that he had collected all of them.

Donavan realized that this wasn't going to be an easy problem to solve. Maybe no one could help him solve it; maybe he should just give up and get a bigger word jar. Then Donavan remembered the one person who always had the greatest ideas of all. Donavan turned on his side, pulled the covers over his shoulders, and closed his eyes.

When Donavan woke up, the rain was beating a steady rhythm on the windowpanes. He jumped out of bed and looked out his window. Overhead the clouds were like gray, puffy pillows. And when he looked down, he saw lots of umbrellas. There was a large, purple-polka-dotted umbrella, a green–striped one with tiny blue flowers, and a small red umbrella that looked like a poppy. The umbrellas were like a parade of brightly patterned mushrooms. Donavan laughed and began to get dressed.

Donavan went downstairs and saw his mother digging in the hall closet. She seemed to be in a big hurry.

"Good morning, Mom," Donavan said, going over to stand beside her. "What's the big rush?" he asked. His mother didn't seem to be listening. She just dug deeper into the closet.

"It's a perfect day to visit Grandma." Donavan kept talking. "I thought it would be fun to put on my new raincoat and stomp in some puddles."

"Not today, Donavan, I need you to be a good big brother and do me a favor." Donavan's mom pulled a shiny black raincoat from the closet and put it on as she talked.

"But, Mom, this is important. I've got to see Grandma today."

"Honey," she said, buttoning up her coat, "you are going to have to do your something important later in the day. Nikki has a terrible cold, and I want her to stay in bed."

"I thought Dad was going to be home today." Donavan really wanted to see his grandmother.

"He is, but your father is down in the basement working on the sign for his shop. He can't have any interruptions. He needs peace and quiet so that he can concentrate," Donavan's mom said firmly.

"Maybe I could just go around to Grandma's and make it quick?" he insisted.

"Donavan, I would let you do that

if I could, but I have got to get a copy of your father's business card to the printer. If I don't, our order won't be finished in time." Donavan's mom put her hands on his shoulders and said, "Honey, all of us have to help get ready for the opening. You do want to help out, don't you?" she asked.

"Yes, Mom," Donavan answered.

"You stay with Nikki until lunchtime, and then, if your father is finished, you can go and visit your grandmother," his mother said firmly. She picked up her big canvas bag and green umbrella and headed for the front door. "Donavan, don't you leave this house until your father says it's okay," she said before closing the front door.

"Yes, ma'am," he said to the empty room.

Donavan stared at the splattered windowpanes until he saw his mother's umbrella disappear around the corner.

"Well, I guess I'm stuck in the house," Donavan said with a long sigh.

5

DONAVAN'S DELAY

Donavan opened the door to Nikki's room and peeped in. She was sitting cross-legged in the middle of her bed, surrounded by stuffed animals, toys, books, and games. On her lap sat a large box of tissues. Nikki looked sleepy and squinty eyed.

"My nose won't breathe right," she complained. Her voice came out funny, and Donavan laughed. "What's so funny?" she asked.

"Nikki," Donavan said, plopping down on her bed, "you've got the snuffles."

She laughed and asked, "Donnie, is that a real word?"

"Yes, it is." Donavan always had to tell Nikki things. Sometimes he didn't mind, especially when his mother reminded him that he was two years older than his sister was. And that Nikki was just starting school.

"Hey, Nikki. What do you want to do today?" Donavan asked.

"I dunno, anything, I guess," she said sniffling loudly. Nikki didn't really seem to care. "Maybe we could go downstairs and look at cartoons?"

"Nah, Mom wants you to stay in

bed. Besides, I'm supposed to keep you company, not the TV."

"Maybe we could color in my new coloring book?" Nikki suggested.

"Nope, that's a baby thing to do, and besides, you always take the good pages," Donavan answered, bouncing on the bed. "Come on, think of something, Nikki," he said.

"I can't think if you rush me," Nikki whined. "Donnie, you don't want to do anything I say." She looked like she was going to be sad.

"Okay, okay. I'll do what you want, but it's gotta be fun," he said.

"Donnie?" Nikki asked hesitantly. "Could we look at some of your words?"

"Why?" Donavan asked suspiciously.

"'Cause, they might make me feel better."

"How?" he asked, not quite believing her.

" 'Cause, they would cheer me up and make me laugh, and then I would feel better," she explained, looking at him and wrinkling her nose.

"You really think so?" Donavan wasn't convinced.

"Yup, and, Donnie, I want some silly words, some happy words, and maybe some get-well words. And if you have any magic words, I want them too."

"You can pick a word," Donavan said slowly, trying to think it over. "But you can't keep it. You have to put it back in my jar." He waited to see if Nikki would agree.

"Okay," she said, smiling.

Donavan got off the bed and slowly went to the door. Just before he closed the door, Nikki sneezed loudly. Donavan smiled. He had just put the word

GESUNDHEIT into his jar. That would be the perfect word for Nikki to pick!

★　★　★

When Donavan came back into Nikki's room, he carried the word jar under his arm. He set the jar down on the bed very carefully. He took his time because he wanted Nikki to know that his word jar was important to him. He took the top off and said, "Pick a word, Nikki, and then give it to me. I'll tell you what it means."

Nikki closed her eyes and picked a slip of paper from the jar. When Donavan took the paper from her, he read the word and smiled. This was going to be fun. He popped a tissue from Nikki's box and waved it in front of her nose. "ABRACADABRA," he said in a loud voice. Nikki looked at Donavan. He was acting so crazy, she couldn't figure out what he meant.

"ABRACADABRA," he said again and touched the tip of her nose with the tissue. She still looked puzzled, so Donavan decided to give Nikki a hint. "ABRACADABRA, cold go away," he said, only louder this time.

"Is it magic?" she asked.

"You're right, ABRACADABRA is a magic word to make things appear or disappear. I just made your cold disappear!" Donavan said laughing. "Now pick another word."

"I feel better already," Nikki said, closing her eyes and reaching into the jar.

6

DONAVAN'S DEPARTURE

Donavan was reading when he heard his father's footsteps in the hall. He got up from his chair and tiptoed across the room. He didn't want Nikki to wake up. They had played with his words until she picked the word LULLABY. To give her a hint, Donavan sang her a song. Nikki was so tired from playing that she fell asleep.

Donavan's father opened the door and peeped into Nikki's room. Donavan put his finger to his lips to keep his father from speaking. He picked up his jar and followed his father down the stairs and into the kitchen.

"How are you doing, partner?" his father asked.

"Fine, and Nikki's feeling a lot better," Donavan said quickly. Before his father could ask another question, Donavan rushed on. "Can I go over to Grandma's and visit? It's really important." Donavan didn't want to waste another minute. He had had fun keeping Nikki company, but now he wanted to get his problem solved.

"Okay, but you watch yourself crossing the streets in the rain," his dad said. "And Donavan, why don't you

slicker drizzle rainy

chef cookery giz

ask your Grandma if she's free to come to dinner tonight? Tell her I'm doing the cooking," he added.

"I will," Donavan called over his shoulder. He was already pulling on his shiny green slicker, rain hat, and his yellow rubber boots. He tucked his word jar in the crook of his arm. He thought if his grandma could see his problem, it might help her to come up with a great idea. Donavan opened the kitchen door and stepped out into the steady drizzle.

7

DONAVAN DINES

Donavan pushed open the heavy glass doors to the Mellow View Apartments. He smiled at Mr. Bill Gut, the security guard, as he signed his name in the guest book. Donavan pushed the button and got onto the elevator. His grandma lived on the fourth floor. Donavan didn't like where Grandma lived now. Everyone there seemed so gloomy. He wondered if all senior citizens' apartment buildings were like that. He missed the big house that Grandma used to live in, with its front porch and large backyard. Grandma had decided that her old house was too large after Grandpop died, so she sold it and moved. Now Grandma lived in the senior citizens' building just a few blocks from where Donavan lived. He could see her anytime he wanted, and that was the best thing about her new apartment.

Donavan knocked on the apartment door and waited. When his grandma opened the door and saw him, she smiled.

"Donnie! What a pleasant surprise,"

Grandma said, opening the door wider. "It's nice to see you. Come in."

Donavan went inside and began to take off his coat. He looked around Grandma's apartment. His grandma was a collector, too. She collected anything given to her by her family and friends. Donavan thought this was a silly idea the first time she explained it to him. But then he decided that he liked the way Grandma's different collections blended together. Her apartment reminded him of a patchwork quilt—colorful, warm, and cozy. Old-fashioned dolls in lace-trimmed dresses were propped against an assortment of pretty teapots. Strange seashells of different shapes and sizes surrounded potted philodendron, ivy, and African violets in small clay pots. Tin cans with faded labels from long, long ago shared a shelf with tiny ceramic animals. Grandma also collected fancy old hats. She had a large felt hat with lots of peacock feathers. Another hat was box-shaped and covered with a veil. The veil was sprinkled with lots of glittery stars. In the bands of some of her hats, Grandma had stuck postcards friends had sent her from faraway places. One postcard invited her to "Sunny, funny Acapulco." Another postcard said that things were just "Dandy in Dixieland."

Donavan's favorite place in Grandma's apartment was her picture wall. Here she displayed photographs of people she knew and liked. Grandma said that if she had not seen a person for a long time, she would visit them on her wall. So whenever he missed his grandpop, Donavan would go to the wall and visit him.

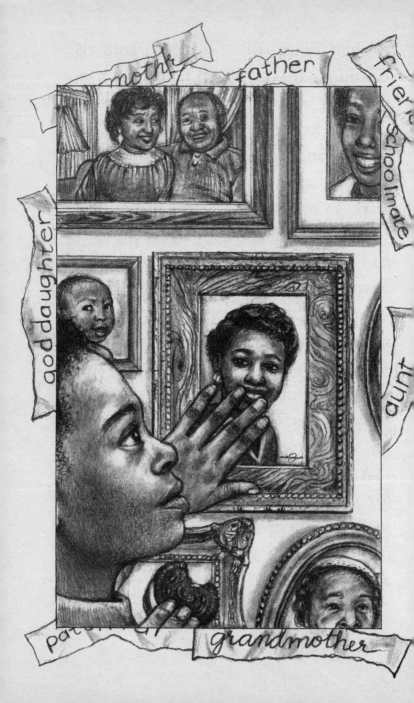

"Donnie," Grandma called from the kitchen, "would you like to have some lunch?"

"Is it soup?" Donavan loved Grandma's soup.

"Yes, it's your favorite, and I have plenty of crackers," Grandma answered. "Did you call your dad and let him know that you got here safely?" Grandma asked.

"Not yet, I'm getting ready to do it now. I'll tell Dad I'm staying for lunch," Donavan said. He wondered which of his favorite soups Grandma had fixed, he had so many.

8

DONAVAN'S DISAPPOINTMENT

After lunch, Donavan set his jar on the dining room table and explained his problem to his grandma. When he finished talking, he sat back in his chair and waited for her solution.

Grandma reached over and plucked a few slips of paper from Donavan's jar. She looked at a slip of paper and laughed.

"Donnie," Grandma said, "do you remember when Pooh traded your ice-cream cone for a broken kite?"

"I won't ever forget that," Donavan said, frowning. Grandma showed him the word BAMBOOZLE, and they both laughed. "And this word EMPORIUM," Grandma said shaking her head slowly. "It makes me think of long ago, when I was a young girl. I used to buy licorice at Mr. McCready's store." She selected another word from the jar. "Donnie, where did you get this word?" she asked. She was surprised to see KALEI-DOSCOPE written on the slip of paper. "I haven't seen one of those in years. I wonder if kids still play with them."

"I have never seen a kaleidoscope,

Grandma, but I saw a picture of one in an old catalog. That's where I found the word," Donavan answered.

Grandma read several more words before she looked at Donavan over the rims of her wire glasses.

"Donnie," she said, "you sure have got yourself a treasure here. This is a wonderful collection of words." Donavan smiled and sat up a little straighter.

Grandma's praise made him feel good, but Donavan still needed a solution to his problem.

"Do you see my problem, Grandma?" he asked. "I thought of getting a larger jar, but that would only get full, too."

"Well, honey, what do other collectors do when their collections grow too large?" she asked.

"I dunno," Donavan said. He thought about it for a minute. "Well,

Pooh collects buttons, but he never gets too many because he trades them for other things.''

"Like what?" Grandma asked.

"Sometimes he trades for a poster, or for a few comics. Once he traded three buttons for a T-shirt," Donavan explained.

"You think you could do that?" Grandma asked.

"No, Grandma, I can't think of anything I could get worth my words," he said. "And I really don't want to give any of my words away," he added.

Grandma settled back in her chair. She didn't say anything for a long while, and Donavan began to feel a little uneasy. Maybe, just maybe, his grandma didn't have a solution. She dipped her hand back into the word jar and pulled out a few more words.

"There are some words in this jar

that I know folks living here could use," she said. Donavan slipped to the edge of his chair and wondered what his grandma was going to say. She continued.

"Now, I like the word PERSNICKETY. That word fits Miz Marylou to a T. That woman has to have everything she does just right." Grandma slipped another word from the jar. "CANTANKEROUS—that's a perfect word for our guard, Bill Gut. I'll bet he argues with flies."

Grandma laughed and Donavan joined in. He loved the sound of his grandma's laughter. After they caught their breaths, Grandma said, "I enjoyed your words, Donnie. I'm sure a lot of people would." She smiled at him and waited to see if he had something to say.

"Grandma, I'd be glad to let any of

ollection   amass   ...ues

emporium   ...cumulation

your friends see my words. But they couldn't keep them—I'd have to have them back for my collection." Donavan's voice was firm.

"Well, I am sorry if I didn't help you."

"Oh, Grandma, that's okay," Donavan answered, trying hard not to show his disappointment. He did not want to hurt his grandma's feelings. "Besides," he said getting up from the table, "if we don't have a solution today, maybe you'll think of something tomorrow."

Grandma helped him with his boots, hat, and coat. Donavan picked up his word jar and tucked it firmly under his arm. Grandma walked with him to the door.

"Take care of yourself, 'Word-gatherer,' " she said, hugging him close.

9

DONAVAN'S DIPLOMACY

In the elevator, Donavan thought about his word jar. It had taken months, weeks, days, and hours to fill it. Deciding which words to keep was hard. Then Donavan checked the spelling and made sure he understood what each new word meant. What had his grandma been thinking of? It seemed like she wanted him to just give his words away. He loved his word collection. But he had to think of a way to handle it, now that it was growing so large.

The elevator doors opened, and Donavan stepped into the lounge. He saw three of Grandma's neighbors sitting around the television set. They didn't seem to care much what was on. And there was Mr. Perkins, sitting by the window, looking at the raindrops hitting the windowpane. Miss Millie had a magazine opened on her lap, but she wasn't reading it. Mr. Crawford, the mailman, was sitting on a hassock rubbing his feet. He looked as if he couldn't take another step. No one in the room was talking to or looking at each other, except Miz Marylou and Mr. Bill Gut. They were standing at the security guard's desk arguing very loudly. No one else was paying any attention to them. As Donavan walked closer he could hear every word they said.

"Miz Marylou, this lounge will open or close when I say so," Mr. Bill Gut said in a gruff voice.

"Well, I am telling you, Bill, that's a mistake. That should be decided by the people who live here," she answered back.

"I'm the guard, and I say what goes on in this lounge," Mr. Bill Gut bellowed.

"Well, I live here and I say that people who live here should set the time," Miz Marylou said almost as loudly.

Donavan looked from one to the other. They both began to shout at the same time, since neither one was listening to what the other was saying. Donavan set his word jar on the corner of the desk and dug around inside the jar until he found a certain word. He tugged Miz Marylou's sleeve and then Mr. Bill's jacket. They both looked down, surprised to see Donavan standing there.

"I think you two need this word," Donavan said in a stern voice.

They both looked at the yellow slip of paper in Donavan's hand. Miz Marylou giggled, and Mr. Bill Gut smiled.

"Well, Marylou, what time do you think is a good time to open?" Mr. Bill Gut asked, scratching his head.

"Bill, I checked with a couple of people and they suggested ten o'clock. What do you think of that?" Miz Marylou asked, smiling at Mr. Bill Gut.

Donavan let out a loud sigh of relief. He had come at just the right time—they needed the word COMPROMISE.

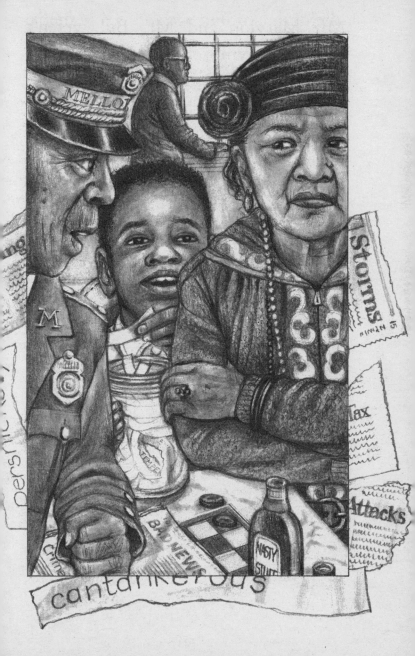

Miz Marylou and Mr. Bill weren't shouting anymore. They were talking to each other quietly; they were coming to an agreement. That sure made Donavan feel good. His word had been just what they needed.

Donavan suddenly remembered that his father had asked him to invite Grandma to dinner. He ran back to the elevator and pushed the UP button.

10

DONAVAN'S DELIGHT

"Back so soon?" Grandma asked, opening the door. "I thought you had gone home."

"I forgot to invite you to dinner tonight. Dad is going to cook. Do you want to come around?" Donavan asked.

It didn't take Grandma long to make up her mind. She loved Donavan's father's cooking.

"Well, I certainly do—in fact, why don't I just get my coat and walk with you?" Grandma suggested. "Maybe we could talk about your word jar a little bit more," she said.

Donavan waited while Grandma got her coat and locked her apartment door. She was carrying a big brown paper sack, and he wondered what was in it. As they walked down the hall, Donavan began to tell Grandma about how he had helped Miz Marylou and Mr. Bill Gut.

When Grandma and Donavan got to the lounge, Donavan could not believe what he saw. Grandma's neighbors were up and around, laughing and talking. They all seemed excited. He looked around to see what was going on.

Donavan saw that they were waving little yellow slips of paper in their hands.

"MY WORDS! THEY HAVE MY WORDS!" Donavan shouted.

Some people had one slip of paper in their hands, others had two. Mr. Avery was no longer slumped in front of the TV. He was tacking one of Donavan's words up on the bulletin board. Miss Millie was looking up the word on her slip of paper in a pocket dictionary. Donavan looked over at the desk and saw Mrs. Agnes digging into his word jar. There were people in a line behind her laughing and talking. They were waiting to get a word from his jar.

"WHAT'S GOING ON?" Donavan asked, as loud as he could. "GRANDMA! STOP THEM. THEY ARE TAKING MY WORDS!" He

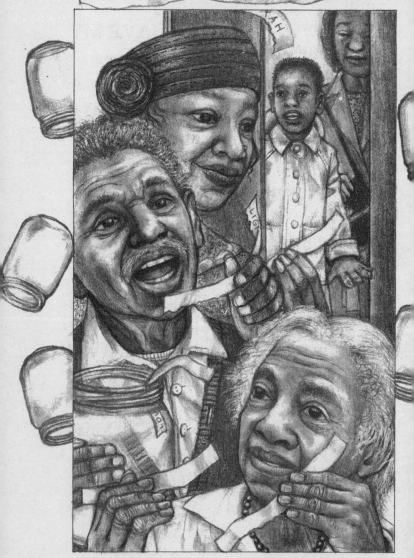

felicity

turned to his grandma, but she looked just as surprised as he felt.

"Donnie, calm down. They didn't know. You left the jar on the desk," she said in a quiet voice.

"I AM GOING TO GET MY WORD JAR," Donavan said firmly. "EXCUSE ME," he shouted. "EXCUSE ME, MAY I GET PAST?" he yelled, moving through the crowd. He pushed a little, he even shoved a bit. It was no use. Donavan couldn't stop what was happening.

Mr. Crawford, the mailman, passed Donavan and waved his word over his head. "PERSEVERANCE," he called out. "That's just the word I need. Some days I get so tired, I can hardly make it. I'm going to try just a little harder to keep going," he said, tucking the word in his shirt pocket.

Donavan stopped pushing and stood still.

"Wow! One of my words made Mr. Crawford feel better," Donavan said. He looked around and saw Miss Millie talking to Mr. Foote. Donavan was surprised.

"BOISTEROUS," he heard Miss Millie say in her soft voice. Grandma always told Donavan that Miss Millie was so shy that she hardly ever spoke to anyone.

Mr. Foote, on the other hand, spoke to everyone. "Well, I'll be darned," Mr. Foote said in surprise. "My word is TIMID!"

"Perhaps we should exchange words," Miss Millie suggested.

"Oh, no. Maybe I need to quiet down some. Sometimes I am a bit loud," Mr. Foote said softly.

"You're right, I think I'll keep my

word too. I am going to start speaking to people more. I am going to change my ways." Miss Millie's voice sounded like she meant it.

"Did my words do that, make them want to change?" Donavan asked himself in surprise.

All around him, Grandma's neighbors were laughing and talking to each other. They had never acted so lively before.

"Nikki was right. Words can make people feel better," Donavan said quietly.

"Donavan!" Miz Marylou called out, as she walked over and stood next to him. "Your words are wonderful. I just couldn't help myself, after you gave Bill and me a word, I . . . I . . . well, I got carried away. I just gave Mr. Kincaid the word LEISURE. That man works entirely too hard," she said smiling.

"And Donavan, people just started coming up and asking for words, and if they didn't get one they wanted, they just traded it." She looked so pleased, it was hard for Donavan not to smile.

Mr. Bill Gut came over and pinched Donavan's cheeks. Mr. Perkins patted his shoulders. Eveyone wanted to thank him for sharing his words. Donavan felt as if the sun had come out inside him. Mr. Bill Gut pointed to the empty jar on the desk and said, "Looks like we cleaned you out, young fellow."

When Grandma pushed through the crowd, she looked worried.

"Donnie, are all of your words gone?" she asked. "Honey, I am so sorry, I know you didn't want to give your words away. Maybe you could ask for them back?" she said.

Donavan looked up at her and smiled.

"Grandma, they love my words, the words made them talk to each other. Look," he said, pointing to Mr. Foote and Miss Millie. "They are talking to each other." Donavan was so excited. "And Grandma, Mr. Crawford the mailman doesn't look so tired anymore." Grandma looked around the room and smiled.

"Donnie, you know, Mr. Mike got the word CHORTLE, and I actually heard him giggle," she said laughing. "But, Donnie, they didn't give you anything for your words." Grandma was still worried.

"Yes, they did. They made me feel like a magician. My words changed them." The sunshine Donavan felt inside was shining all over his face.

Grandma set the large paper sack she had been carrying on the desk and pulled a large glass jar from it. Donavan stopped smiling and caught his breath. "Grandpop's humidor!" he exclaimed. No one had been allowed to touch the cigar jar when Grandpop had been alive. No one except Donavan and Grandpop himself. Donavan would climb up on his grandpop's lap and lean over and pull a long cigar from the jar. And then, very carefully, Donavan would put the wooden lid back on.

Grandma wrote on a slip of paper, removed the wooden lid from the jar, and dropped the paper in.

"This is for you, 'Wordgatherer,' " Grandma said, her voice full of pride.

Donavan took the slip of paper from the jar. On one side it said "A happy accident," and on the other side the word SERENDIPITY was written.

Donavan looked around. Everyone was watching his grandma and him. He hugged Grandma until it hurt. He would be proud to put his word collection in his grandpop's jar. Donavan was going to have a wonderful time collecting new words. It would take hours, days, weeks, and maybe even months. But the next time his jar filled up, he would not have a problem. It would be fun finding new ways to give his words away.